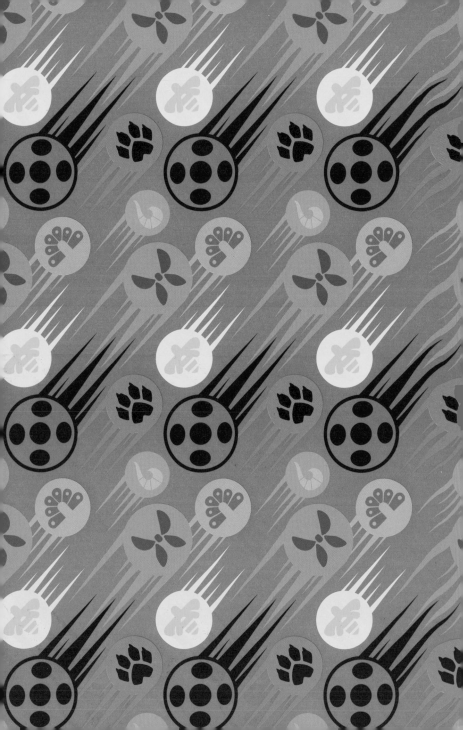

Superhero Origins

Little, Brown and Company
Hachette Book Group
1290 Avenue of the Americas, New York, NY 10104
Visit us at LBYR.com

First Edition: September 2022

Little, Brown and Company is a division of Hachette Book Group, Inc. The Little, Brown name and logo are trademarks of Hachette Book Group, Inc.

The publisher is not responsible for websites (or their content) that are not owned by the publisher.

Library of Congress Control Number: 2020947473

ISBNs: 978-0-316-70668-1 (pbk.), 978-0-316-70671-1 (ebook)

PRINTED IN CHINA

APS

10 9 8 7 6 5 4 3 2 1

Superhero Origins

Adapted by Christy Webster

LITTLE, BROWN AND COMPANY
NEW YORK BOSTON

Chapter 1

Many years ago, magic jewels with great powers were created. These jewels are known as the Miraculouses. Over the centuries, heroes have used the powers of the Miraculouses for the good of the human race. Each Miraculous has a magical connection to a Kwami, a creature who helps the jewel's wearer use its power.

Two of the Miraculouses are more powerful than the others. The first is the earrings of the Ladybug, which give the wearer the power of creation. The second is the ring of the Black Cat, which grants the wearer the power of destruction. According to legend, anyone who controls both at the same time will have absolute power.

• • •

In modern-day Paris, an old man closes his eyes and holds out his hands, ready to bestow a healing treatment on his patient. Just as he is about to begin, he hears a frantic whisper.

"Master! Master!"

It's Wayzz, hovering just behind him. The patient cranes his neck to see what's happening.

Master Fu cannot let anyone see the tiny green Kwami. Instead, he imitates his voice. "Master… master…," he chants. He peers at his patient. "It's part of the treatment."

The client puts his head back down, satisfied with the explanation. Master Fu shoots Wayzz a look that he hopes says, *Get out of sight until we're alone!* Wayzz gets the message and zips behind the phonograph sitting on a nearby dresser.

As soon as Master Fu has finished with his patient, Wayzz appears again. The little Kwami lands in Master Fu's palm, looking frantic.

"Master! It's the Moth Miraculous," Wayzz says. "I felt its aura!"

Master Fu is surprised. "I thought it had been lost forever."

"But, Master," Wayzz continues, "it's a negative

aura. I'm afraid the Miraculous may have been found by a dark power."

This is not good news. If the Moth Miraculous has gotten into the wrong hands, there's no telling what will happen. "We must find Nooroo and his Miraculous," Master Fu says, lifting his own Miraculous, the bracelet of the Turtle. He prepares to transform. He winds up and...doubles over in a coughing fit.

"Please, Master," Wayzz pleads. "You are—"

"Still young!" Master Fu interrupts, raising a finger in protest. "I am only 186 and a half!"

He wanders over to his phonograph. "But you are right, Wayzz. I can no longer do it alone." Pressing the buttons on the device in precise order, Master Fu opens a secret compartment. There, a small box waits for its next hero.

• • •

"Marinette! Your alarm's been going off for fifteen minutes!"

Across town, a teenager named Marinette opens her eyes and sees her phone buzzing away. "Got it, Mom!" she yells, dragging herself out of bed and down the stairs. She kisses her mom good morning and starts to make breakfast.

As she pours chocolate powder into a bowl, Marinette sighs. The first day back at school is always the hardest. "I bet you anything Chloé will be in my class again," she says.

"Four years in a row?" Mom asks. "Is that possible?"

"Definitely," Marinette replies. "Just my luck."

"Don't be so defeated!" Mom says. "It's the start of a new year! I'm sure everything will be just fine."

Marinette nods reluctantly. She sets down the powder, accidentally knocking an orange loose from the fruit bowl. The orange rolls across the counter, bumping into both a baguette and a butter knife and somehow managing to knock over a container of milk and a cup of yogurt. Marinette's shoulders slump.

Before she leaves for Collège Françoise Dupont, her dad hands her a box of beautiful green macarons from his bakery.

"Thank you, Dad!" Marinette squeals. "My class will love them!" Then she kisses both her parents goodbye and hurries out the door.

At the first crosswalk, Marinette is waiting for the light when she sees a little old man, hunched over his cane as he crosses the busy street. He's not even looking for cars! Marinette doesn't hesitate—she leaps into traffic to help the man to the sidewalk, just in time to avoid an oncoming car.

Unfortunately, her box of macarons also ends up on the sidewalk. Several of them tumble out and crumble beneath the feet of people walking by.

"What a disaster," the man says.

"Don't worry. I'm no stranger to disaster," Marinette says. "Besides, there are still a few left."

The man takes one of the remaining macarons from the box and bites into it. "Delicious!"

A school bell rings in the distance. Marinette is going to be late on the very first day! She says a quick, polite goodbye and runs off with the box. The man smiles as she disappears.

Marinette makes it to class and takes her

regular seat in the second row. Unfortunately, the first person to greet her is the last person she wants to see.

Chloé Bourgeois's hand slams down on Marinette's desk. "This is my seat," she barks.

"This has always been *my* seat," Marinette replies. Suddenly, Sabrina Raincomprix, Chloé's snooty sidekick, slides into the space next to her.

"Not this year," Sabrina sneers. "New school year, new seats."

"That's Adrien's seat," Chloé says, pointing to the spot in front of Marinette. "So *this* is going to be my seat."

"Who's Adrien?" Marinette asks.

Chloé and Sabrina both laugh. "Only a famous model," Sabrina says.

"And *my* best friend," Chloé adds. "So…move!"

"Who made you the queen of seats?"

Marinette turns to find the source of the

voice. There's a new girl holding a phone and standing right in front of Chloé. She has glasses and red ombré hair. "Come on," she says, taking Marinette's arm and leading her to the front row. Marinette manages to drop even more macarons on her way.

"Sorry!" she cries.

"No biggie!" the new girl assures her.

"I wish I could handle Chloé the way you do," Marinette says, sighing.

"You mean the way Majestia does it!" The girl shows Marinette the comic she's been reading on her phone. A strong superhero in a colorful costume hovers over a cityscape

on the screen. "She says all that is necessary for the triumph of evil is that good people do nothing. You just need more confidence, uh…"

Marinette takes the last macaron out of the box, splits it in two, and hands half to her new seatmate. "Marinette," she says.

"Alya," the girl says. They eat their macaron halves and smile as Miss Bustier, the teacher, starts class.

Maybe this year won't be so bad.

● ● ●

Outside the school, a teenage boy with a huge mop of blond hair leaps up the steps toward the entrance. An expensive car swerves to a stop, and a woman steps out. "Adrien, please!" she calls. "You know what your father wants!"

Adrien turns and faces his father's assistant. "But this is what *I* want!" He gears up for a big argument, but before it can begin, he spots an old man sprawled on the sidewalk nearby. The man has dropped his cane. It's lying in the street, just out of his reach. Adrien could just slip into the school—he's probably late already—but he decides to take a quick detour first.

He hurries down the stairs, picks up the cane, and hands it to the man.

"Thank you," the man says.

Adrien smiles, but when he turns around, his father's employees are standing between him and the only place he wants to go—school. He won't be able to get past them. They lead him to the car.

"Please don't tell my father about this," Adrien says with a sigh.

• • •

Back inside, the bell rings. Students make their way to their next class. Marinette notices that Chloé is pouting—probably because her "best friend" never made it. But before Marinette has a chance to think more about this mysterious Adrien, her thoughts are interrupted.

"Kim!"

Marinette turns around. Her classmate Ivan Bruel looks furious. He's crushing a piece of paper in his giant fist and glaring at Kim Chiến Lê, who grins in response. Just as Ivan draws back his arm to punch the other boy, Miss Bustier's sharp voice cuts in.

"Ivan! Go calm down in the principal's office,"

she says. Ivan stalks out of the room, grumbling.

• • •

Far away, a dark figure surrounded by butterflies watches the scene. He sees all Ivan's negative emotions pouring out—anger, sadness. It's the perfect opportunity to set the next phase of his plan in motion.

The dark figure speaks. "Burn a hole into his heart, my horrible akuma."

He closes his hands around a white butterfly and transforms it into a dark-purple moth with bright-white edges. It disappears out the window.

"Fly away, my little akuma!" he calls after the creature. "Evilize him!"

The moth flies over Paris in search of its target. It flutters through a window of the school, where Ivan has just entered the principal's office.

• • •

"Hasn't anyone ever taught you to knock?" scolds

Mr. Damocles, making Ivan even angrier than he was before. Ivan steps back out of the room, closes the door, and prepares to knock. That's when the evil moth lands right on his hand, turning his crumpled piece of paper an inky black.

Out of nowhere comes a booming voice—one only Ivan can hear. *"Stoneheart, I am Hawk Moth,"* it says. *"I give you the power to seek revenge on those who have wronged you!"*

"Okay, Hawk Moth," Ivan says, smiling for the first time that day.

• • •

Meanwhile, Marinette and Alya arrive in the library just as a huge crash rumbles the room, knocking Marinette off her feet. Alya helps her up, and they run to the security screens to see what's going on.

Marinette can't believe her eyes. Outside the school, a giant monster is stomping around, smashing the sidewalks to bits. The monster looks as if it's made of solid rock.

Chapter 2

Marinette watches the stone giant stomp away. "*Kim!*" it cries. Somehow it sounds like Ivan's voice.

"What's going on?" Marinette asks no one in particular.

"It's as if he's been transformed into a real-life supervillain!" Alya says. Marinette turns to look at her. Alya almost seems excited about this.

Alya takes out her phone, checks the GPS and battery, and hurries away.

"Where are you going?" Marinette calls after her.

"Wherever there's a supervillain, a superhero has to be close behind. No way I'm missing this!" Alya says, sprinting out the double doors.

• • •

A few blocks away, Adrien sits in his father's huge mansion, forcing himself to participate in a private tutoring lesson.

"Who was the first president of the Fifth French Republic?" Nathalie asks.

Adrien sighs. He could be learning this at school. With other kids his age. "Everyone thinks it was Charles de Gaulle," he replies. "But it was actually René Coty."

Just then, to Adrien's surprise, his father enters the room.

"Leave us alone, would you, Nathalie?" his father says to his assistant. Nathalie hurries out.

This can't be good. Adrien is almost never alone with his father—especially in the middle of a weekday. His father's usually too busy running his fashion empire.

His father doesn't keep him in suspense for long. "I've already told you—you are *not* going to school."

So Nathalie did tell on him after all. "But, Father—"

"I will not have you out there in that dangerous world!"

"It's not dangerous!" Adrien argues. "I just want to make friends like everybody else."

"You are *not* like everyone else!" His father is practically shouting now. "You are my son!"

Adrien watches his father stalk out of the room and send Nathalie back in. She starts to speak, but Adrien doesn't let her finish. He runs to his bedroom instead.

Adrien flops onto the bed. If he can't go to school, he might as well sulk for the rest of the day.

BOOM! BOOM! BOOM!

Adrien's whole room shakes. He rushes outside to see what's going on. Sirens are blaring, and loud footsteps thunder down the cobblestone streets. Adrien hurries back inside and turns on the TV. First, he sees the mayor encouraging everyone to stay home. Then the news cuts to footage of a huge stone man picking up cars, smashing them, and getting even bigger as he destroys everything around him.

"As incredible as it seems," a flustered reporter says into the camera, "it's being confirmed that a supervillain is attacking the city of Paris."

Adrien can't believe it. He has to look away from the screen to gather his thoughts. But just

then, his eyes land on a strange box resting on his coffee table. He's never seen anything like it. It's small and black, with red markings that glow—as if by magic.

"What's this doing here?" he asks.

• • •

"What's this doing here?" Marinette says in her own room across town. After coming home to watch the news coverage of the supervillain, she's found a mysterious little box sitting on her desk.

When she cracks it open, she's blinded by a bright burst of red light. As the light fades, a tiny creature appears, hovering in the air before her eyes.

Marinette screams and backs away. "A giant

bug! Or…a mouse! A bug mouse?"

"Don't be scared!" the creature says, coming closer. It's red, with a black spot on its forehead and big, bright eyes.

"Bug mouse talks!" Marinette screams while throwing everything she can get her hands on at it.

The creature dodges every object. "Listen, Marinette—"

Marinette finally grabs an empty glass from her vanity and brings it down over the little creature, trapping it inside.

"What are you?" Marinette asks. "And how do you know my name?"

"I am a Kwami," it replies. It doesn't look like anything Marinette has ever seen before, but it has the sweetest little voice. "My name is Tikki. Now let me explain...."

• • •

Adrien's box also contains a Kwami, a tiny black creature with pointed ears and bright-green eyes. His name is Plagg. While Tikki is explaining herself to Marinette, Plagg is trying to eat every object in Adrien's room. Just as Plagg's chomping down on the TV remote, Adrien finally manages to grab him.

"I still don't know what you're doing here," Adrien says.

"Look, I grant powers," Plagg says blandly. "Yours is the power of destruction. Got it?"

Adrien shakes his head.

• • •

"The power of creation?" Marinette asks. This is just too much. She opens the door to call her parents up to help.

"No! You have to trust me," Tikki pleads. "No

one else can ever know I exist."

"This has to be a mistake," Marinette says. "The only superpower I could have is super-awkwardness. You should go see Alya. She loves superheroes!"

Tikki shakes her head. "*You're* the chosen one. You're the only one who can stop Stoneheart." She shows Marinette a pair of red earrings waiting for her in the magic box. They look like ordinary studs with black spots. Marinette sighs and puts them on.

"All you have to do is capture the akuma," Tikki explains. "Use your Lucky Charm—that's your secret superpower!"

"This is all going too fast, Tikki," Marinette says.

"Trust yourself," Tikki says confidently. "Just say 'spots on'!"

"Spots on?" Marinette asks. In an instant,

everything starts to change. A strange energy flows through her. Tikki disappears into Marinette's earrings, and Marinette begins to transform. When it's all over, she looks down and sees that her whole body is covered in skintight red-and-black fabric. She looks in the mirror. There is a spotted mask over her eyes. Tikki is nowhere to be seen.

Marinette tugs at the suit. It won't come off.

"Tikki!" she calls out. "If you can hear me, I want my normal clothes back! I'm not going anywhe—"

Just then, Marinette sees the news. The reporters are following Stoneheart across the city toward Montparnasse Tower. As he stomps through the streets, Marinette looks closer. There, following just behind him, is a girl on a bicycle. She has red ombré hair and glasses.

"Alya?" Marinette says with a sigh. She decides

she can't waste any more time. As strange as this superhero stuff seems, she must try to help her friend.

"Marinette, did you get home okay?" her mom calls from downstairs.

"Uh…just super!" Marinette calls back while climbing out onto the rooftop patio so her mom won't find her.

Marinette tries to collect her thoughts. "Okay, I have special powers," she tells herself. She touches her hip. There's a gizmo there, red with black spots just like the rest of her gear. She pulls it out and plays with it a little. "And…this super yo-yo thing?"

She tries giving it a toss. It zips away from her hand and toward the spire of Notre-Dame, blocks away. It twirls around a gargoyle's head, its cord stretching all the way back to Marinette.

Marinette gives the cord a gentle tug, and she's

29

yanked into the air, zooming across Paris.

"Ahhhhhh!"

As she hurtles toward the ground, Marinette grabs the first thing she sees—a boy her age balancing on a wire. She knocks him off balance, and they both go tumbling to the pavement. Luckily, her cord snags a lamppost just in time to catch them before they crash. Once they're safe and sound, Marinette takes a good look at the boy she collided with. He's in head-to-toe black, with a gold bell at his neck, cat ears, and…an eye mask?

She's found another superhero.

"Hey there," he says. "I'm, uh…Cat Noir."

Chapter 3

Marinette doesn't know what to say. She can't give her real name while she's dressed like this. Superheroes are supposed to have superhero names!

"I bet you're the partner my Kwami told me about," Cat Noir says.

"I'm Ma—" Marinette tries to pull her yo-yo down from above. The gizmo lands on her head and bounces to the ground. "I'm madly clumsy," she finishes.

"I'm learning the
ropes, too," Cat Noir
says, just as a tower
crumbles into
rubble a few blocks

away. Without hesitating, he
pulls out a staff and leaps into action.

Marinette watches as Cat Noir lunges over the
nearest building, chasing after the monster. "Wait,
where are you going?" she calls out.

"To save Paris, right?" Cat Noir replies before
pouncing out of sight.

Marinette looks down at the red-and-black
yo-yo in her hand. She thinks of Tikki and
what the Kwami said right before Marinette's
transformation. "Trust yourself," she mutters to
herself. Then she winds up and tosses her yo-yo
again, this time on purpose.

When she finds Cat Noir, he's landing in a

soccer stadium where Stoneheart is chasing her classmate Kim.

"Kim!" the monster thunders. "Who's the wuss now?"

Cat Noir leaps between them as Kim scurries away. "It's not very nice to pick on people who are smaller than you," he quips.

"I guess you're talking about yourself?" Stoneheart roars. He lunges to attack. Marinette watches as Cat Noir dodges, using his metal staff to vault over the monster and return his attacks. It looks like he can make the staff longer and shorter, depending on what he needs it for. But every time Cat Noir gets a hit in, Stoneheart grows larger and angrier. He grabs Cat Noir in his giant, stony fist.

"Where are you, partner?" Cat Noir calls out.

Marinette knows he's talking about her. She's supposed to help defeat Stoneheart. That's what

Tikki said. But she just doesn't know if she can do it. That's when she hears another voice.

"What are you waiting for, super red bug? The world is watching you!"

Marinette turns and sees Alya. She's filming the fight with her phone, but she's looking straight at Marinette.

Alya was brave enough to follow the monster without any superpowers. She said that evil triumphs when good people do nothing.

Tikki said to trust herself.

She *will* trust herself.

Marinette tosses her yo-yo at Stoneheart. It wraps around his ankles. She swings, slides across the soccer field, and twists the line *just* so—Stoneheart loses his balance and falls to the ground. Cat Noir is free from his grasp.

"Animal cruelty?" Marinette says. "How shame-ful!"

Cat Noir starts to run back into battle, but Marinette stops him with a tug of his tail-like belt. "Wait!" she says. "Haven't you noticed? He gets bigger and stronger with every attack. We need to try something different."

"Okay, then," Cat Noir says. "Let's use our powers. *Cataclysm!*"

Marinette watches as Cat Noir's hand exudes a strange, dark power.

"Apparently, I destroy everything I touch," he explains.

"I don't need a superpower to do that," Marinette mutters. Cat Noir reaches out and touches the goal post. The entire goal turns black, then disappears into nothingness.

"Cool!" Cat Noir says. He breaks into a run toward Stoneheart.

"Wait!" Marinette cries.

With a dramatic flourish, Cat Noir touches Stoneheart's foot.

Nothing happens.

"I guess I only get one shot to use my power," he says, smiling up at Stoneheart. The monster slams him back toward Marinette.

"And you only have five minutes before you change back," she says. "Didn't your Kwami explain?"

"I guess I was a little excited and didn't get all the instructions," he replies.

Marinette looks at Stoneheart. Her special power is the only thing they have left. She braces herself. She doesn't know what's about to happen.

"Lucky Charm!" she cries. Her yo-yo explodes into countless little ladybugs. They swarm together and form…another spotted red suit? It hangs limp in Marinette's hands.

"*Super* power," Cat Noir says sarcastically.

Marinette thinks through the problem. Tikki said she had to capture the akuma. Where could it be?

Stoneheart barrels toward them, preparing to attack. He's made of stone from head to toe. There's nowhere for the akuma to be hiding, except…

"His right hand!" Marinette says. "He never opens it!" The akuma has to be hidden inside.

"So what's your plan?" Cat Noir asks. Marinette quickly takes in her surroundings. She sees the suit her Lucky Charm gave her. She sees Stoneheart's hand—shut tight. She sees Alya filming the whole scene. She sees a water tap and a long hose.

"This," Marinette replies. She grabs the hose and attaches it to the extra suit. "Trust me." She zips her yo-yo around Cat Noir's ankles and spins him, letting him go just in time to fly at Stoneheart and land in his left fist.

"Catch me if you can!" she calls out, leaping toward Stoneheart with the extra suit in hand. With Cat Noir grasped tight in Stoneheart's left fist, the only way for him to catch Marinette is to open his right. As he grabs her, a tiny object falls out onto the field.

Now Marinette and Cat Noir are both in Stoneheart's clutches. "Alya!" Marinette calls out. "The tap!" Alya hurries to the spout and opens the tap. Water flows through the hose and fills the suit Marinette is holding. The suit expands, forcing Stoneheart's fingers apart and giving Marinette enough room to escape the villain's fist.

She lands on the field and races to the object Stoneheart dropped. With a stomp of her foot, it turns to paper and the akuma is released. It flutters away.

Stoneheart disappears in a cloud, leaving

Marinette, Ivan, and Cat Noir alone on the field.

"You were incredible, Miss…Bug Lady!" Cat Noir cheers. "You did it!"

"*We* did it…partner," Marinette replies. She gives him a fist bump and notices that a single bright dot is blinking on his magic ring. That must mean their time is about to run out. "You should get going. Our identities *must* remain secret."

Cat Noir looks at his ring and nods. "Let's do this again soon!" he calls as he bounces out of the stadium.

"Not *too* soon, I hope," Marinette says to herself. She turns her attention to the crumpled paper where the akuma was hiding. It's a note. It says:

YOU HAVEN'T EVEN GOT THE GUTS TO TELL MYLÈNE YOU LOVE HER, WUSS!

Marinette turns to Ivan. He looks so sad.

"Kim wrote it," he admits. "He's always making fun of me."

Marinette puts a hand on his shoulder. "There's no shame in telling someone you love them, Ivan."

"How do you know my name?" he asks. Marinette realizes she's still in costume...and on camera.

"Uncanny! Amazing! Spectacular!" Alya cheers, her phone trained on Marinette and Ivan. She starts grilling Marinette with questions about her superpowers.

Marinette realizes she has to get out of there. She can't be seen when her time runs out. Without another word, she starts to leave.

"Wait!" Alya cries. "I have so many questions, Miss...uh..."

Marinette turns around. "Ladybug," she says. "Call me Ladybug."

Chapter 4

Back home, Marinette watches the news report on the defeat of Stoneheart—and Paris's newest superheroes, Ladybug and Cat Noir.

"I did it," she whispers to Tikki as the Kwami zips around Marinette's head.

She doesn't have much time to celebrate, though. A news flash reports that countless people have been transformed into Stoneheart statues all over the city. They are completely still, but no one knows how long they'll stay that way.

Marinette is stunned. She thought they'd defeated Stoneheart when he changed back into Ivan.

"Did you capture the akuma?" Tikki asks.

The akuma! She released it from Stoneheart's grasp, but she didn't capture it herself. "What does that have to do with these other stone beings?"

"An akuma can multiply," Tikki explains. "If Ivan loses control of his emotions again, he could turn back into Stoneheart—and he'll bring the others to life to serve as his army."

Marinette is devastated. "This is all my fault," she says. "I'm not cut out to be a superhero. Cat Noir will be better off without me."

"Only you can capture the akumas and repair the damage done by villains," Tikki explains. "Cat Noir can't do it alone."

"Then find another Ladybug," Marinette says, reaching for the earrings.

"No!" Tikki protests. But as soon as the earrings are out of Marinette's ears, Tikki is gone.

Marinette feels a small pang of regret, but she knows this is the right decision. She would just make things worse, as she did today.

Still, the next morning before school, she slips the earrings into her bag. Just in case.

• • •

Meanwhile, Adrien has made another break for it. His father will be furious, but today he's going to school—for real this time.

"You're such a strange kid," Plagg remarks. He's floating in front of Adrien's face even as Adrien runs full speed toward school.

"I've had enough of being shut up at home," Adrien explains. "I want to meet people and make friends!"

Plagg slows down. "I'm feeling weak," he says, in an obvious ploy to get more cheese. Ever since they got home last night, he's been gobbling every speck of smelly Camembert Adrien can get from the chef.

"If you want to be able to transform into a superhero, stinky cheese is the deal, my friend."

Adrien is starting to worry they'll both smell like cheese thanks to Plagg's eating habits. But he hands him a wedge of Camembert anyway,

 before sprinting into the school with Plagg hidden in his pocket.

• • •

As they walk through the school's doorway, Alya shows Marinette her new blog: the *Ladyblog*. It's where she's been posting everything she's learned about Paris's newest superhero, Ladybug.

"Check out the number of views since I posted the video!" Alya brags.

"But…what if Ladybug's not really cut out to be a superhero?" Marinette asks.

"What are you talking about, girl? Oh, wait!" Alya narrows her eyes and comes closer. "I know what this is about."

Marinette gasps. She wasn't supposed to let anyone know her secret! How could she be so careless?

"You're scared!" Alya declares. "But don't be. I've seen her. Ladybug is a true superheroine."

Marinette smiles. Alya is so confident. And she knows everything about superheroes. Marinette touches her bag where the earrings are hidden, an idea forming.

"So you really don't remember anything?" a voice rings out. Marinette and Alya turn to see a group of kids crowded around Ivan. They're grilling him about the events of the day before.

"You were seriously out to crush me, dude!" Kim says.

"It was *soooooo* cool," another student says.

Marinette notices Mylène Haprèle standing a few feet back from the crowd. Ivan looks at Mylène, but she looks the other way.

"I have no idea! I

wasn't myself, I guess." Ivan says.

"Once a monster, always a monster," Chloé sneers.

Ivan stands up, clearly annoyed. He stalks away from the crowd.

"Don't let the door hit you on the way out!" Chloé calls after him.

"How could you say that?" Alya asks.

"Ooh, she's mad," Chloé taunts. "Look out! Maybe she'll turn into a monster, too!"

"Hey, Chloé."

At the sound of this new voice, Chloé's whole mood changes. She breaks into a run and throws her arms around the newcomer. "Adri-kins!" she cries.

The other students start crowding around Chloé and the new kid. Marinette takes the chance to go talk to Ivan.

She finds him by the lockers, headphones

blasting. She touches his arm to get his attention.

"You know," she begins, "you should tell Mylène how you feel."

"I don't know what you're talking about," Ivan protests.

"I saw the way you look at her," Marinette says, smiling.

Ivan grunts unhappily. Marinette scrambles to turn it around. If he gets upset, he might wake the statues.

"No negative emotions!" she blurts. "I mean, be positive! Go talk to her!"

"I'm no good with words," Ivan says.

"You could draw her a picture," Marinette offers. "Or send her flowers…"

"I could write her a song?" Ivan suggests.

Marinette is surprised. She didn't know Ivan was a songwriter. "What girl wouldn't love a song written especially for her?"

Ivan takes out a pen and paper. Marinette thinks he might actually look happy.

The bell rings. "Uh…just stay positive!" she says before hurrying to class.

• • •

In Adrien's new classroom, his childhood friend Chloé shows him where to sit. "I saved this seat for you," she brags.

Adrien can't wait to meet new people. He introduces himself to the first kid he sees, who looks wary.

"So you're friends with Chloé, then?" the kid asks.

Adrien turns to look back at Chloé. She and her friend Sabrina are putting chewed gum on a seat in the front row.

"Hey!" he says, going over to them. "What's that all about?"

"The brats who sat here yesterday need a little attitude adjustment," Chloé explains. "I'm just commanding a bit of respect."

"Do you think that's really necessary?" Adrien pokes at the gum, trying to get it off the seat.

Chloé rolls her eyes. "You have a lot to learn about this school, Adri-kins."

• • •

When Marinette finds Alya again, she works up the courage to ask her a big question. "Would you like to be a superhero? Fight monsters and villains?"

"Totally!" Alya replies without hesitation. "I'm not scared of anyone. Why?"

It's the answer Marinette was hoping for. "No reason," she says, slipping the earring box into Alya's bag. Finally, Ladybug is out of her hands. Alya will find the earrings, put them on, and then *she'll* be Ladybug. Someone who can really handle it.

Just as she feels relief for the first time in days, Marinette walks into class and sees Chloé's friend—the new kid—messing with her seat!

"Hey!" she cries angrily. "What are you doing?" She sees a big wad of gum stuck to the seat.

Chloé and Sabrina burst into laughter.

"Oh, I get it," Marinette says. "Very funny, you three." Just what she needs this week—another bully.

"No!" the boy says. "I was just trying to get this off!"

Marinette nudges him out of the way so she can cover the gum with a tissue. She turns and looks at the new boy. "You're friends with Chloé, right?"

"Why do people keep saying that?" he mutters.

Marinette sits down, carefully avoiding the gum.

She slumps in her seat. It didn't take long for things to get back to normal around here. She glares at the new kid as he takes his seat across the aisle. Now that she gets a good look, he seems familiar.

"I know I've seen him somewhere before," she says.

Alya holds up her phone. It's the cover of a fashion magazine. A tall boy with a mop of blond hair shows off a stylish outfit. It's the same kid!

"Of course!" Marinette says, swiping through more covers on the screen. "He's the son of my favorite fashion designer!"

"Daddy's boy, teen supermodel, *and* Chloé's buddy?" Alya says, laughing. "Forget it."

Adrien's first day at school isn't going so well.

"Why didn't you tell her it was Chloé's idea?" the kid next to him whispers.

"I know she's not perfect, but I can't throw her

under the bus," Adrien says miserably. "She's, like, my only friend. I've known her since I was a kid."

"Time for you to make some new friends, dude." The boy sticks out his hand to shake. "I'm Nino."

• • •

Back by the lockers, Ivan has finally finished his song for Mylène. He waits outside the girls' bathroom. When she comes out, he hits play on his phone.

"I made this for you," he says. Face-melting metal music blasts from the speaker. He takes a deep breath and starts singing...or screaming. *"Mylène!"*

Mylène runs away, her fingers stuck in her ears. Ivan stops singing and sadly looks down at his page of lyrics. She didn't like the song. He only managed to scare her away.

As he sulks, his sadness gives way to anger.

He crumples the paper in his fist, drops his phone to the ground, and stomps on the screen. He doesn't see the purple moth appear through the window and flutter into his fist again. But he does hear the booming voice of Hawk Moth, loud and clear.

"This is your second chance, Stoneheart. This time you have extra help," it says. *"Nothing will keep you from the love of your life. Just remember, I need something in return."*

In his mind's eye, Ivan sees a pair of spotted red earrings and a black ring with an acid-yellow paw print. Then he feels a familiar power coursing through him.

Across Paris, the stone statues come alive.

Chapter 5

*M*ylène!" Stoneheart smashes through the classroom door, screaming. Students scatter as he finds who he's looking for and picks her up in his stony fist.

"Let go of me, Ivan!" Mylène cries.

"I'm not Ivan!" the monster roars. "I'm Stoneheart. You and I are going to be together… forever!"

"Daddy, the monster is back!" Chloé wails into her phone. Stoneheart grabs her, too, and smashes through the wall of the classroom. He jumps onto the street and stomps away, leaving a trail of crushed pavement and rubble in his wake.

Alya is ready. "Come on! Let's follow him."

Marinette shakes her head. "You go," she says. "I'm finding myself a safe place to hide."

"You'll miss Ladybug in action!" Alya argues.

Marinette closes her eyes. It hurts to give up Ladybug and leave Alya on her own, but she has to try to get the power into the right hands. She picks up Alya's bag and holds it out to her. "You and Ladybug will both be fine without me."

Alya shrugs and sprints out of the room.

"Wait! Your bag!" Marinette calls after her. Knowing she can't abandon her friend, Marinette takes the bag and chases after Alya.

She catches up in a narrow alley a few blocks away. She sees Cat Noir battling three stone monsters while Alya films the action on her phone.

"If you can hear me, Ladybug, I could use a little help!" Cat Noir yells out as a monster tries to smash him with a car.

Alya looks around. "What's she waiting for?" she mutters. Just then, a monster tosses another car. Cat Noir throws his staff to intercept it, but the car crashes into a nearby building and pins Alya to the wall. "Help!" she cries.

One of the monsters grabs Cat Noir. The two others follow as it starts to stomp away, leaving Cat Noir's staff behind.

Marinette takes in the scene. Alya is trapped. Cat Noir is captured. Stoneheart is on the loose with two of her classmates. There's no one left to help.

And Marinette has the earrings. There's only one thing to do.

She pulls the little box from Alya's bag and puts on the earrings. Tikki appears immediately.

"I knew you'd come around!" she squeals happily.

"I'm still not sure I'm up for this," Marinette says. "But Alya's in danger. Spots on!"

Once she's in costume, Ladybug tosses her yo-yo at the car pinning Alya to the wall. The cord wraps around the car, and she uses her yo-yo to pull it away from the building until her friend has enough room to escape. Then she grabs Cat Noir's staff. "You can't stay here. It's too dangerous," she warns Alya before turning to chase after the monsters.

Bouncing off buildings and swinging around

with her yo-yo, Ladybug finally catches up to them. She lands on top of a lamppost and tosses the staff to Cat Noir, who's still trapped in the monster's giant stony fist. "Extend it!" she calls out. Cat Noir uses the staff's power, snapping it into a longer length and forcing the monster to loosen its grip. He starts to drop to the street below.

Marinette flings her yo-yo at Cat Noir, catching him by the ankle and suspending him from the lamppost, safely out of the monsters' reach.

"Have I ever told you that you turn my world upside down?" Cat Noir says with a wink, dangling by his feet.

"Quite the jokester," Ladybug replies from her perch on the lamppost. The three stone monsters stomp around, roaring with anger. "But your comedic timing needs work."

She unravels her yo-yo and leaps over the nearest building, pulling Cat Noir behind on her yo-yo's string. Soon they're way ahead of the bumbling monsters.

"Aren't we going to take care of them?" Cat Noir asks.

"No, we go to the source," she replies. "That one."

They land on a roof with a view of the Eiffel Tower. The original Stoneheart is standing on the first platform of the tower, roaring with anger as helicopters hover around him. On the ground, a terrifying mob of stone monsters slowly makes its way toward the tower.

"I demand my daughter's safe return!" a voice blasts from a megaphone. Ladybug sees Chloé's father—the mayor—yelling at Stoneheart from a safe distance away.

"Daddy!" Chloé cries from the monster's fist.

"You're welcome to her," Stoneheart says, winding up and throwing Chloé toward the street. The mayor screams. Ladybug leaps into action.

On her way down, Chloé begs for a bit of luck. "Please, I'll be nice to everyone, I pro—"

Ladybug catches Chloé just before she hits the pavement.

"I didn't promise," Chloé says.

"What?" Ladybug asks. But Chloé just runs into her father's arms.

Now Stoneheart is alone with Mylène on the tower. Ladybug and Cat Noir look up, trying to decide what to do next.

"If I'd captured Stoneheart's akuma the first time around, none of this would have happened," Ladybug admits to her partner. "I'm not the right one for the job."

"Without you, Chloé wouldn't be here," Cat Noir says. "We can do this. Trust me, okay?"

Ladybug looks into Cat Noir's eyes. Maybe he's right. Maybe they *can* help…together.

"Okay," she says.

Stoneheart roars. Ladybug and Cat Noir look up again. Then Stoneheart doubles over in a coughing fit. What is happening?

Suddenly, a huge swarm of purple moths erupts from Stoneheart's mouth, and he falls back onto the platform. The swarm slowly forms into a sinister-looking face, floating high above Paris. A booming voice begins to speak.

"*I am Hawk Moth,*" it says. Everyone watches, confused. "*Ladybug and Cat Noir, give me the earrings and the ring now. You've done enough damage.*"

Ladybug does her best slow clap. "Nice try, Hawk Moth," she says. "We know who the bad guy is. Without you, none of these innocent people would have been transformed into villains. We will find you. And you will hand us *your* Miraculous." Then she springs into action. She leaps up the Eiffel Tower and spins her yo-yo around and around the giant face. The face dissolves into nothing as each and every moth is absorbed into Ladybug's yo-yo.

Once she's finished, Ladybug turns back to the crowd, which is watching in awe. "No matter who wants to harm you, Ladybug and Cat Noir will do everything in our power to keep you safe!" she announces to the people of Paris.

Ladybug releases the butterflies—no longer

evil—as people all over the city celebrate.

"Go, Ladybug!" Chloé cheers.

"Whoever she is beneath that mask," Cat Noir says, "I love her!"

While the crowd applauds, Stoneheart lies on the platform of the Eiffel Tower. He still has Mylène in his grasp. Suddenly, he hears Hawk Moth's voice once again.

"They're trying to take your loved one away," Hawk Moth says. *"Snatch their Miraculouses and*

they'll be powerless against you!"

Stoneheart rises to his feet. He's larger than he's ever been, towering over Ladybug and Cat Noir.

"Help me!" Mylène cries from his fist.

"You'll never take her from me!" Stoneheart declares. He heaves his gigantic body up the tower and starts to climb higher, with the group of stone monsters following.

Chapter 6

*L*adybug and Cat Noir watch in horror as the Eiffel Tower is overrun by climbing stone giants.

"We're surrounded!" Cat Noir says. "What do we do now? We can't attack him."

"But we know where the akuma is," Ladybug says. She and Cat Noir look up at Stoneheart. He's high above and climbing higher—one-handed.

"In his clenched fist," Cat Noir says. "The one he's holding Mylène with!"

Ladybug thinks this over. They have to get

Mylène away from Stoneheart. But he won't let go…because he's in love with her.

"That's it!" Ladybug cries. "We don't separate them. We bring them closer together." She throws her yo-yo toward the top of the tower and starts to climb. "They're made for each other! They just don't know it yet."

"I'm not really following, but I guess I better trust you," Cat Noir says, climbing after her. "Something tells me that this is how it's going to be from here on out!"

The two superheroes leap to the top of the

building. Ladybug perches on the spire. Stoneheart is almost to the highest platform.

"Help! I'm scared of heights!" Mylène cries out to Ladybug.

The other monsters start to swarm the top of the tower. Cat Noir prepares for battle. "How are you planning to get them closer than they already are?" he asks Ladybug.

"By using our powers!" she replies. "Lucky Charm!"

She throws her yo-yo high in the air. It explodes into a cloud of ladybugs. They come together to form something that looks like a small red backpack covered in black dots.

Ladybug looks at it more closely. "A parachute?" She doesn't know what to do with it yet, so she straps it to her back.

"Are you sure you know what you're doing?" Cat Noir asks.

"We'll find out soon enough," Ladybug replies. She tosses the yo-yo so that its cord wraps around Stoneheart's head and hand—the one holding Mylène. "Get ready!" Ladybug warns. Then she pulls.

The line tightens, bringing Stoneheart's hand close to his head—close enough that Mylène ends up kissing him right on the cheek! Stoneheart is so surprised that he opens his right fist. Mylène and the akuma both tumble out of his hand and hurtle toward the ground.

Mylène manages to catch hold of the end of one of Stoneheart's fingers. Cat Noir springs into action, leaping down after the akuma and batting it back to the top platform with his staff. This time Ladybug is determined to capture it. But as soon as she releases the fluttering akuma from the crumpled page of lyrics, Stoneheart turns back into Ivan—losing his grip on the edge of the platform. He and Mylène both start to fall.

Ladybug jumps off the tower, leaving the akuma behind. "Cat Noir, you take care of Ivan!" she calls.

"Cataclysm!" Cat Noir shouts. He uses his power of destruction to break an iron bar so that it sticks out horizontally from the tower. He runs across the bar to snatch Ivan out of the air.

At the same time, Ladybug rockets toward the ground. She grabs Mylène midair, rips the cord on the parachute, and whips her yo-yo at the fluttering akuma, capturing it once and for all. She and Mylène drift gently to the pavement.

When she releases the butterfly, it's no longer evil. Ladybug takes off the parachute and tosses it high in the sky. She shouts, "Miraculous Ladybug!"

The parachute explodes into another swarm of ladybugs. They fly over the scene and the city, cleaning up the damage done by the evil akumas. All the stone monsters turn back into people.

"Whoa," Cat Noir says, gawking at the spectacle. "Are you seeing what I'm seeing?"

"Yeah," Ladybug says, with magical ladybugs swirling all around. "It's…miraculous!"

After things settle down, Ladybug makes a suggestion to Ivan and Mylène. "I think you two have some things to talk about."

"Uh…" Ivan looks unsure.

Ladybug hands Mylène the piece of paper the akuma was hiding in. "Maybe it would help if you read the lyrics."

Mylène reads. Her eyes widen. "Wow," she says. "These are really beautiful. It's a shame you can't hear the lyrics when you scre—I mean, sing." She smiles.

"I'm sorry," Ivan says. "I'll be gentle." Mylène surprises him with a big hug.

Ladybug sighs. "They're so meant for each other."

"Like us two," Cat Noir says, reaching out to put his arm around Ladybug. Just then, his ring starts beeping.

"Uh-oh!" Ladybug says, grabbing his hand

before he has a chance to make his move. "Time to split. See you soon, Cat Noir."

"Can't wait," he says.

• • •

The next day on the way to school, Marinette hears Alya's side of the story.

"By the time I biked to the Eiffel Tower, it was all over," she complains.

"Don't worry. You'll get your scoop eventually," Marinette reassures her.

"You're right." Alya straightens her shoulders. "Next target—'Ladybug: An Exclusive Interview!' Or even better—finding out who's really under that mask!"

Marinette laughs. "Good luck with that one."

Inside, Marinette makes a decision. She sets her bag down at her seat in the second row—the one she wanted on the first day—and motions for Alya to sit next to her.

"Wrong seat," Chloé says when she comes in. "Get lost!"

"All that is necessary for the triumph of evil is that good people do nothing," Marinette says, keeping her seat. Alya beams proudly. Chloé scowls. Everyone else in the class laughs—at Chloé. She backs down and takes a different seat, pouting.

"Good job," Alya says.

• • •

Meanwhile, a fancy car approaches the school. Adrien is in the back, video-chatting with his father.

"You will never go back to that school again…," his father says.

"But, Father…"

"Without a bodyguard."

Adrien cheers and leaps out of the car. When he gets to the classroom, he sees Marinette—the girl he accidentally offended with the chewing gum— sitting right behind his seat, where Chloé usually sits. He tries to wave hello, but she sniffs and turns away. She must still be upset.

"Dude, you want to make friends, right?" Nino says. "Talk to her."

• • •

After school, Marinette stands on the front steps, watching the pouring rain. Of course she forgot her umbrella.

"Hey," Adrien says, walking past.

She turns away. She doesn't want anything to do with Chloé or her friends.

"I was only trying to take the chewing gum off your seat," he says, opening a huge umbrella over his head. "I swear."

Marinette looks at him. She's never noticed his big green eyes. They stare into hers.

"I've never had friends before," he says. "This is all sort of new to me."

Then he reaches out to hand her the umbrella.

Marinette doesn't know what to say. She takes the umbrella, her finger brushing against his for just a moment. Then the umbrella closes over her head.

They both laugh. Before she has a chance to form a reply, he runs off into the rainy afternoon.

Marinette waves awkwardly after him. "See— uh—you—uh—why am I stammering?"

Tikki suddenly appears. "I think I might have an idea." She bats her eyes at Marinette.

As Marinette starts toward home, blushing, another umbrella makes its way down the street.

"Excellent choice," Wayzz says to Master Fu, watching the two teenagers go their separate ways.

"Those two are made for each other," Master Fu says. "They just don't know it yet."

83